Good Night Farm

To Bill and Lori – thank you for giving me the opportunity to support your farm.
K.V.

To Anne Berit and Svein – thank you for letting me live on your farm.
H.B

Text copyright © 2020 by Kathleen Vallejos
Illustrations copyright © 2020 by Hanne Brøter
Published by: OAM Press, Hilliard, Ohio 43026
Author Photo: Sarah Huntington
Illustrator Photo: B.T Stokke

Printed in the United States of America
First Printing, 2020

ISBN 978-0-578-75821-3

Ordering Information: This book may be purchased in bulk for promotional, educational, or business use by farms, farmer's markets, agricultural associations, and others.
For details, contact: OAMPress@justthewritething.com

Hilliard, OH 9-2.

Good Night Farm

By Kathleen Vallejos

Illustrations by Hanne Brøter

OAM Press

Dear
Paul Gifford
&
Virginia Laura:
Sweet dreams ♡

Kathleen
Vallejos

Good night to the asparagus
picked first in spring.

Good night to the robin
ready to rest her wings.

Good night to the rhubarb's
red-green stalk.

Good night to the winding trails we walked.

Good night to the strawberries sweet and red.
Good night to the bellies all full and fed.

Good night to the cherries sour and sweet.
Good night to the fruit grown fresh to eat.

Good night to the berries
we call brambles.

Good night to the chickens
whose eggs we'll scramble.

Good night to the blueberries juicy and blue.
Good night to the food colored in every hue.

Good night to the herbs, cucumbers, and greens.
Good night to the squash, tomatoes, and beans.

Good night to the beets that
go deep with their roots.

Good night to the rain,
the mud, and your boots.

Good night to the apples growing on trees.

Good night to the apiary full of bees.

Good night to the Asian pears,
golden, firm, and round.

Good night to the pawpaws
gathered ripe from the ground.

Good night to the mowers,
tractors, and hoes.

Good night to the wagons
parked neatly in rows.

Good night to the peaches, both yellow and white.
Good night to the beautiful rays of sunlight.

Good night to the workers who helped all day.
Good night to the roads that led the way.

Good night to the open
and check in signs.

Good night to the farmers,
it's closing time.

About the Author

Kathleen Vallejos loves children's books and farm-fresh foods, especially those she doesn't have to cook!
She's funny—at least she thinks so—and beloved by her hubby, daughter, and their cats.

About the Illustrator

Hanne Brøter is a Norwegian Graphic Designer and Illustrator. She does illustration work by hand and computer in various styles. Her graphic design and visual branding business is yourbrandvision.com.